THE AMAZING SPIDER-MAN™

THE FUN HOUSE!

by Benjamin Harper
Illustrated by Scott Stewart

Copyright © Marvel 2007. First edition.
Printed in the USA.
All rights reserved.
ISBN: 978-0-696-23478-1

Marvel, Spider-Man: TM and © 2007 Marvel Characters, Inc.
All rights reserved. www.marvel.com
Licensed by Marvel Characters, Inc.

We welcome your comments and suggestions. Write to us at:
Meredith Books, Children's Books,
1716 Locust St., Des Moines,
IA 50309-3023.
meredithbooks.com

It was a big day for Peter Parker! There was a fashion show on the boardwalk at Coney Island. Peter's boss, J. Jonah Jameson, had sent Peter to take photos.

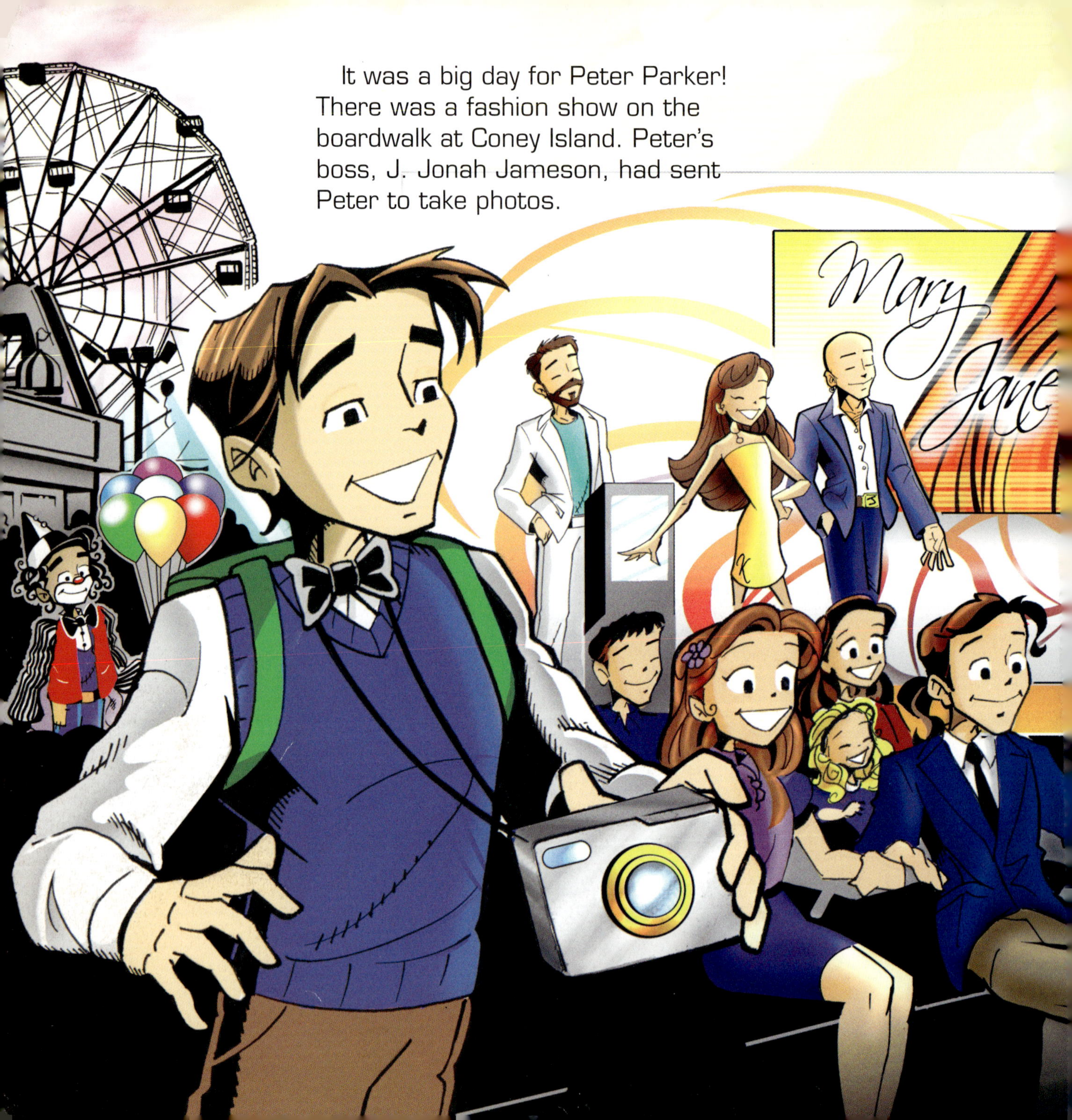
Mary Jane

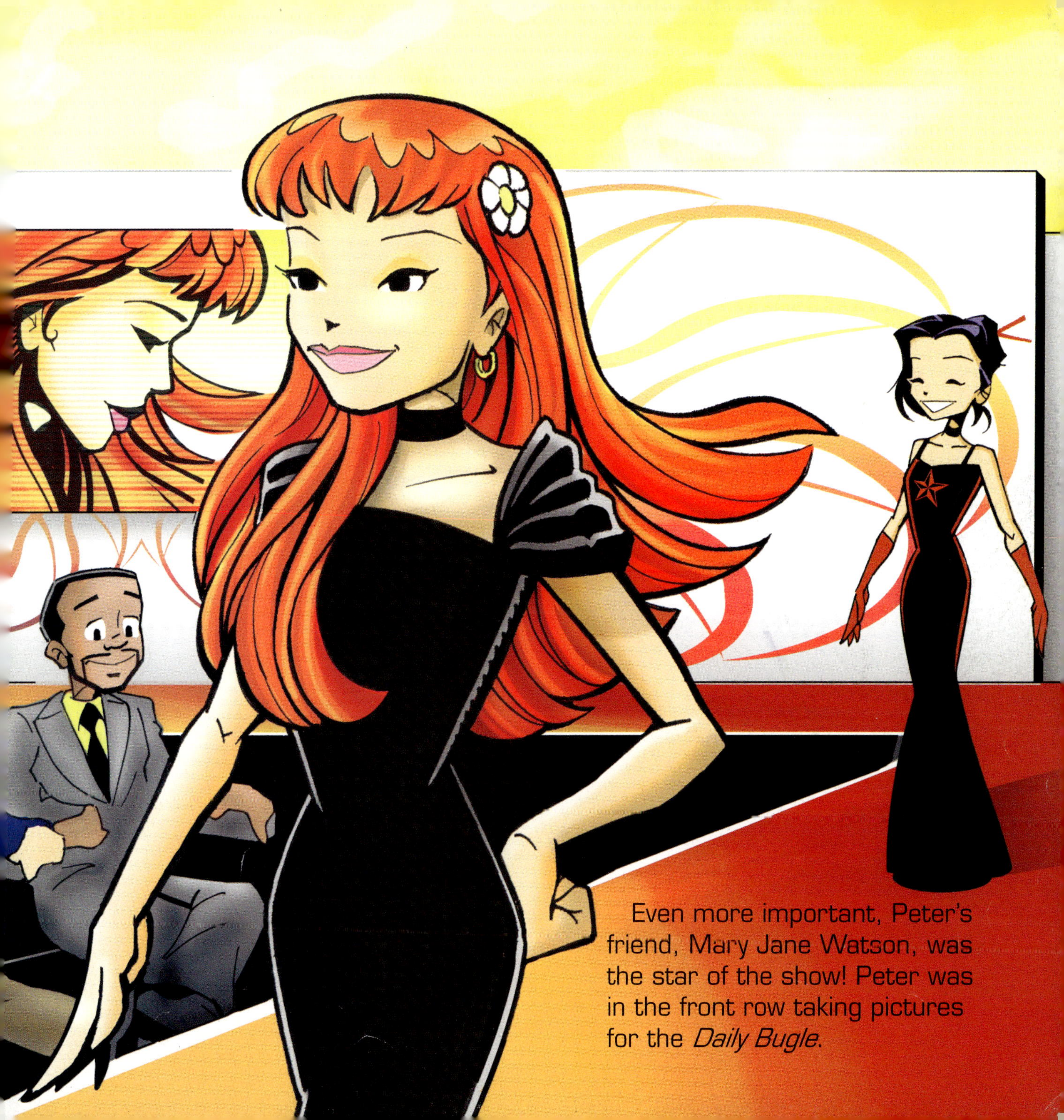

Even more important, Peter's friend, Mary Jane Watson, was the star of the show! Peter was in the front row taking pictures for the *Daily Bugle*.

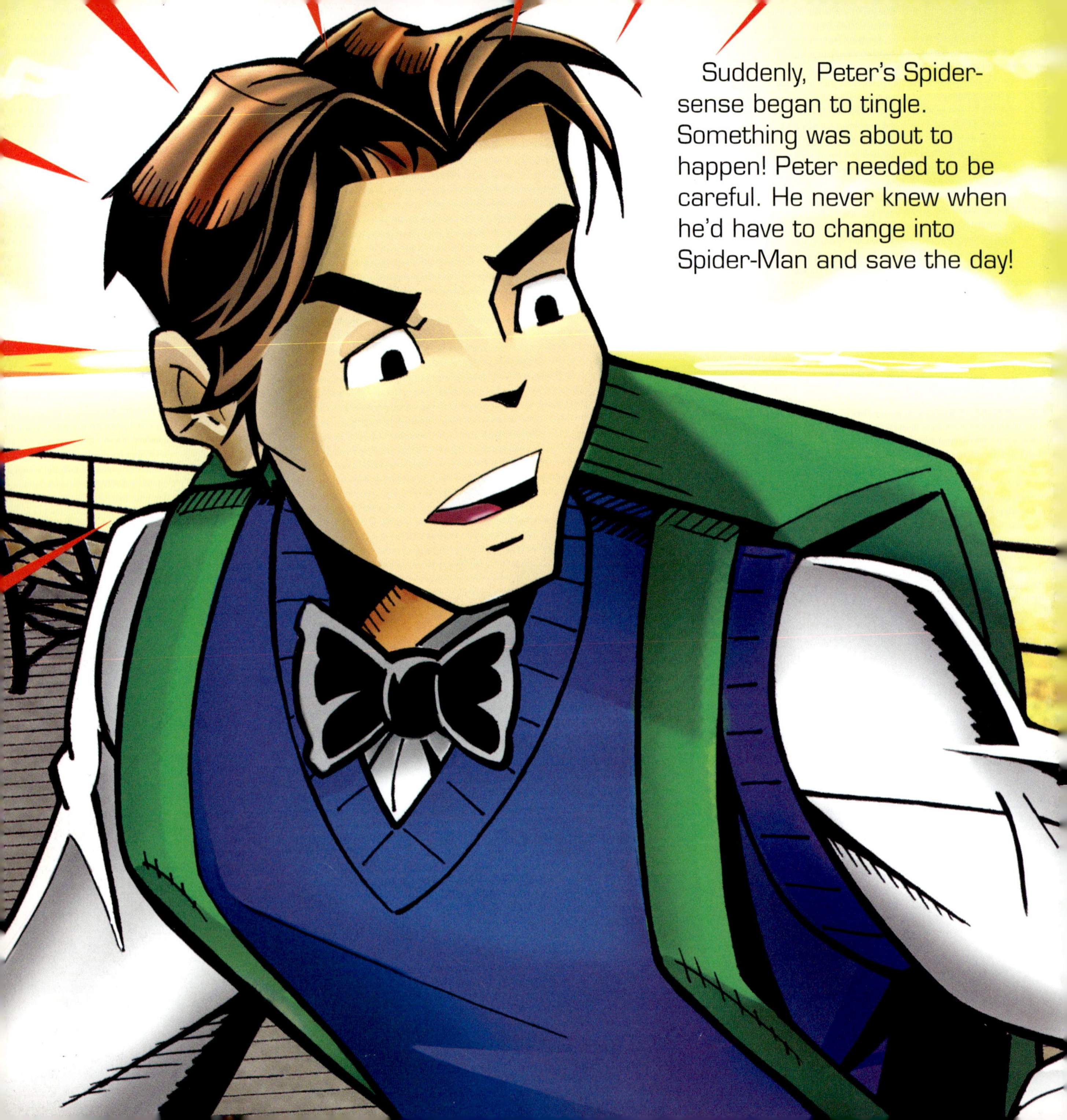

Suddenly, Peter's Spider-sense began to tingle. Something was about to happen! Peter needed to be careful. He never knew when he'd have to change into Spider-Man and save the day!

On the boardwalk everyone was having a great time. Well, almost everyone was having a great time. Sandman, one of Spider-Man's most dangerous enemies—he could change himself into any shape he wanted—was waiting for an opportunity to stir up trouble!

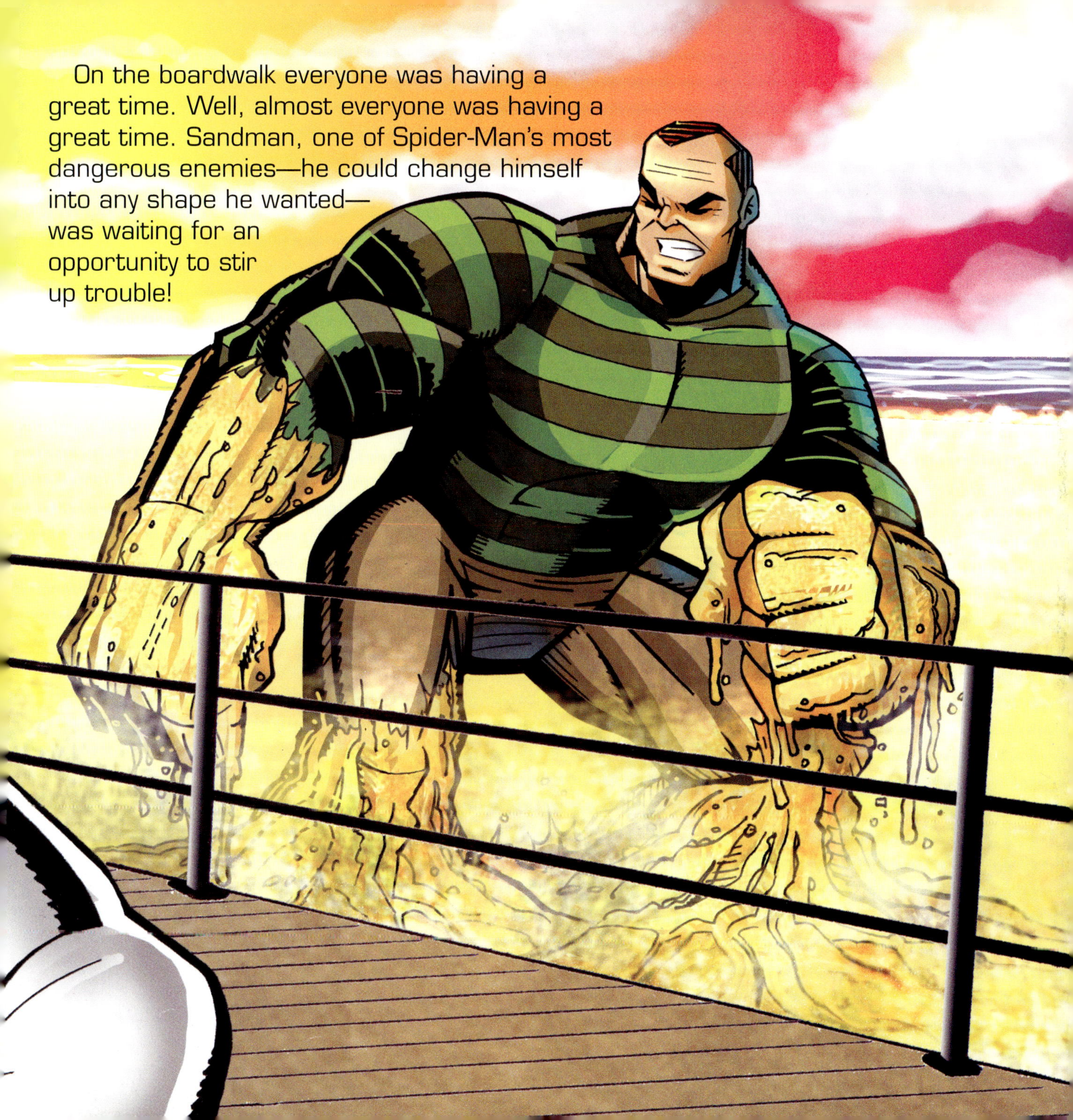

Spider-Man had saved Mary Jane before, and Sandman knew it. He knew he could trick Spider-Man into coming to Coney Island by capturing Mary Jane. When Spider-Man came to her rescue, **BAM!** Sandman would finally get the Webbed One.

Sandman had waited far too long for this!

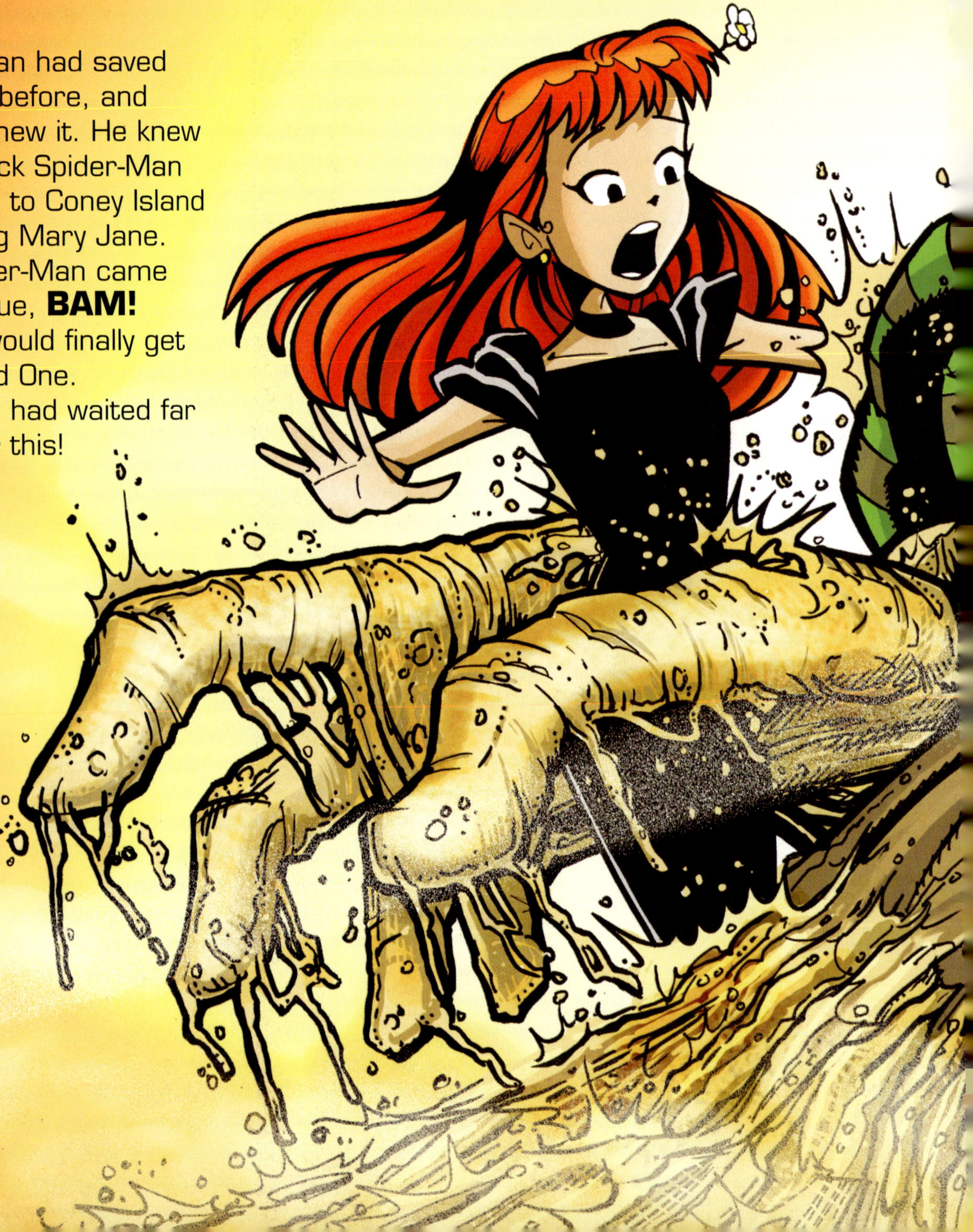

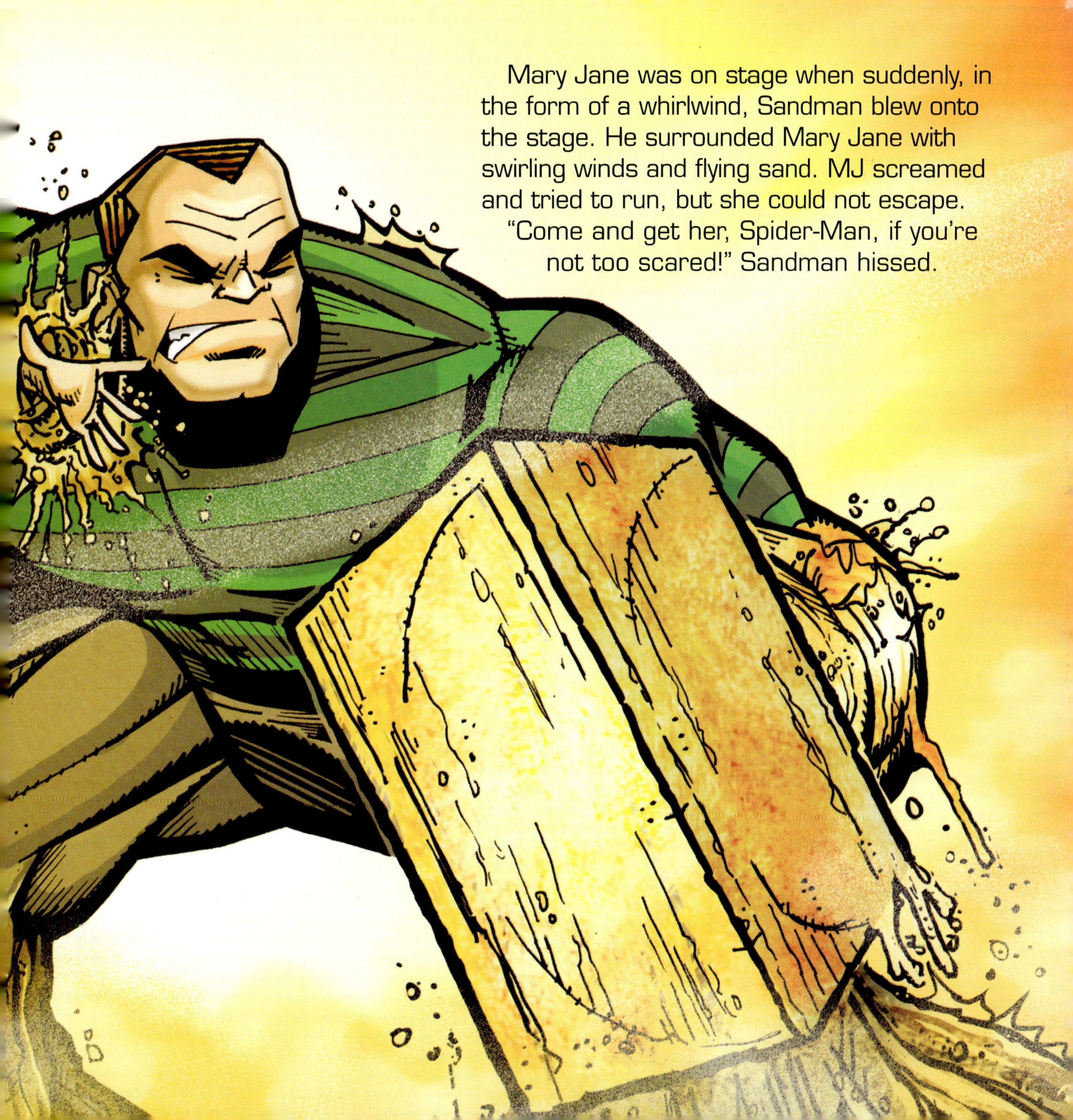

Mary Jane was on stage when suddenly, in the form of a whirlwind, Sandman blew onto the stage. He surrounded Mary Jane with swirling winds and flying sand. MJ screamed and tried to run, but she could not escape.

"Come and get her, Spider-Man, if you're not too scared!" Sandman hissed.

"Let her go, Sandman!" Spider-Man called from a perch high above the stage.

"How'd you get here so fast?" Sandman asked, a little surprised. He released Mary Jane, who stumbled, dizzy from the wind, and ran from the stage.

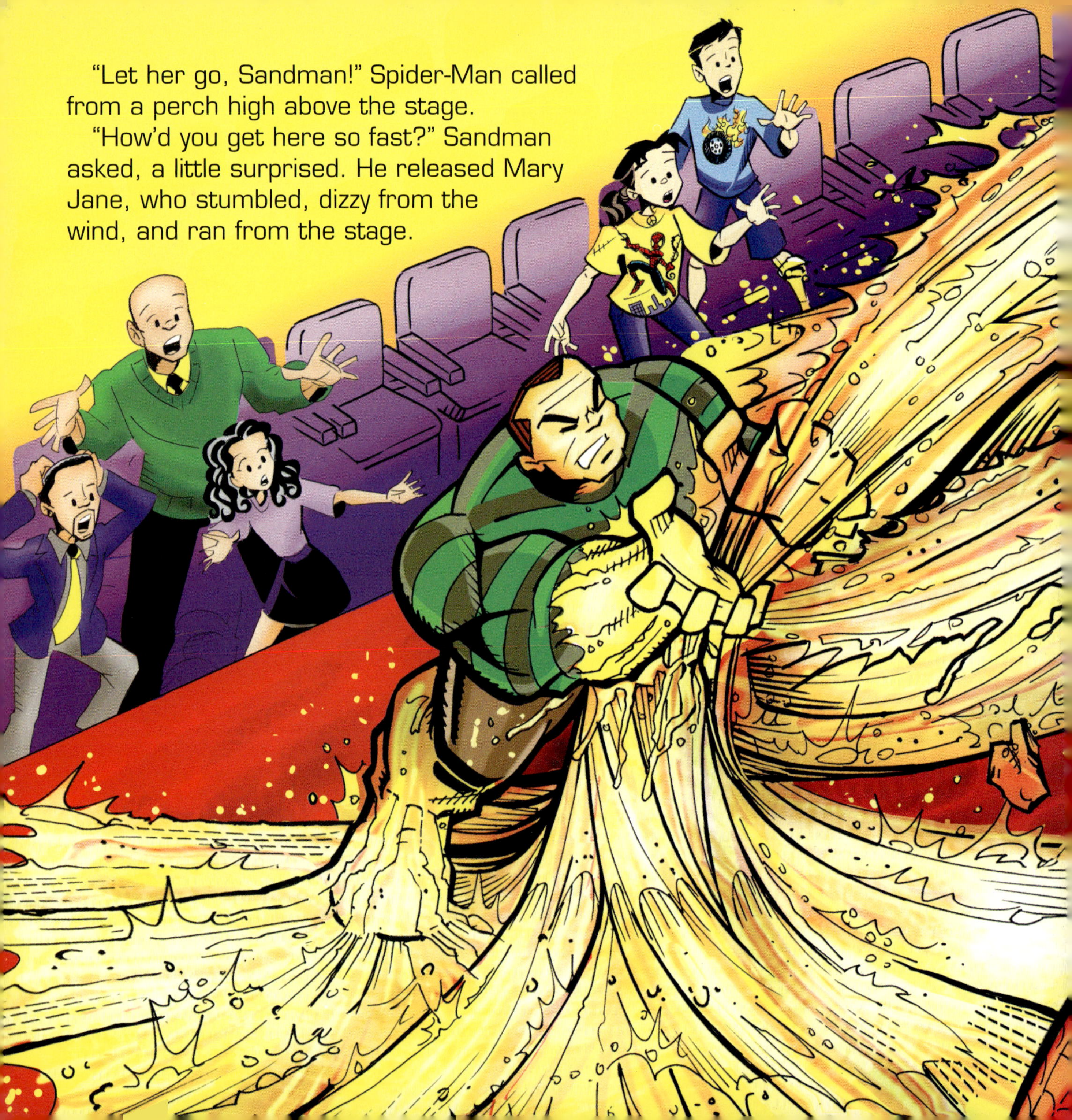

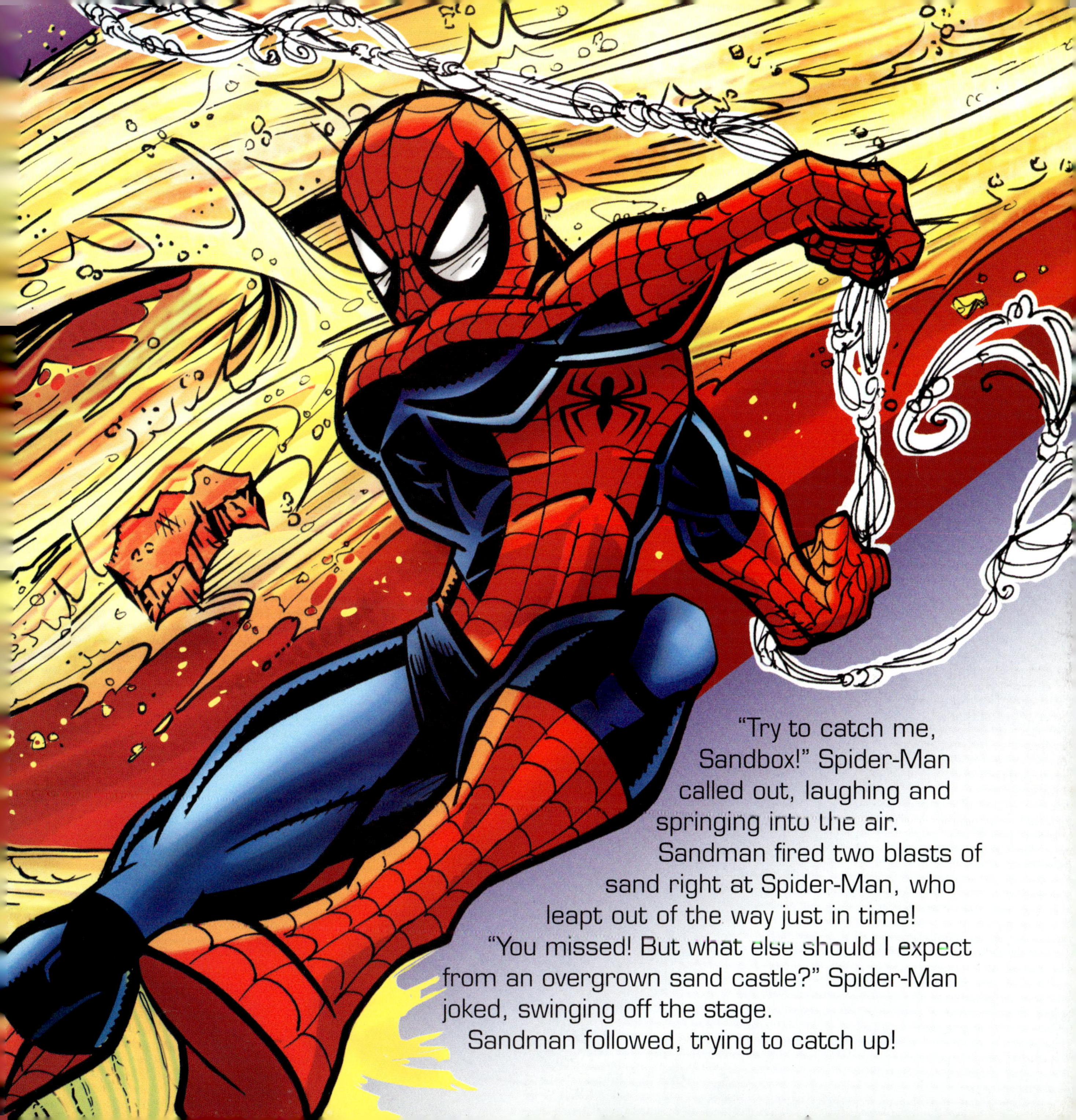

"Try to catch me, Sandbox!" Spider-Man called out, laughing and springing into the air.

Sandman fired two blasts of sand right at Spider-Man, who leapt out of the way just in time!

"You missed! But what else should I expect from an overgrown sand castle?" Spider-Man joked, swinging off the stage.

Sandman followed, trying to catch up!

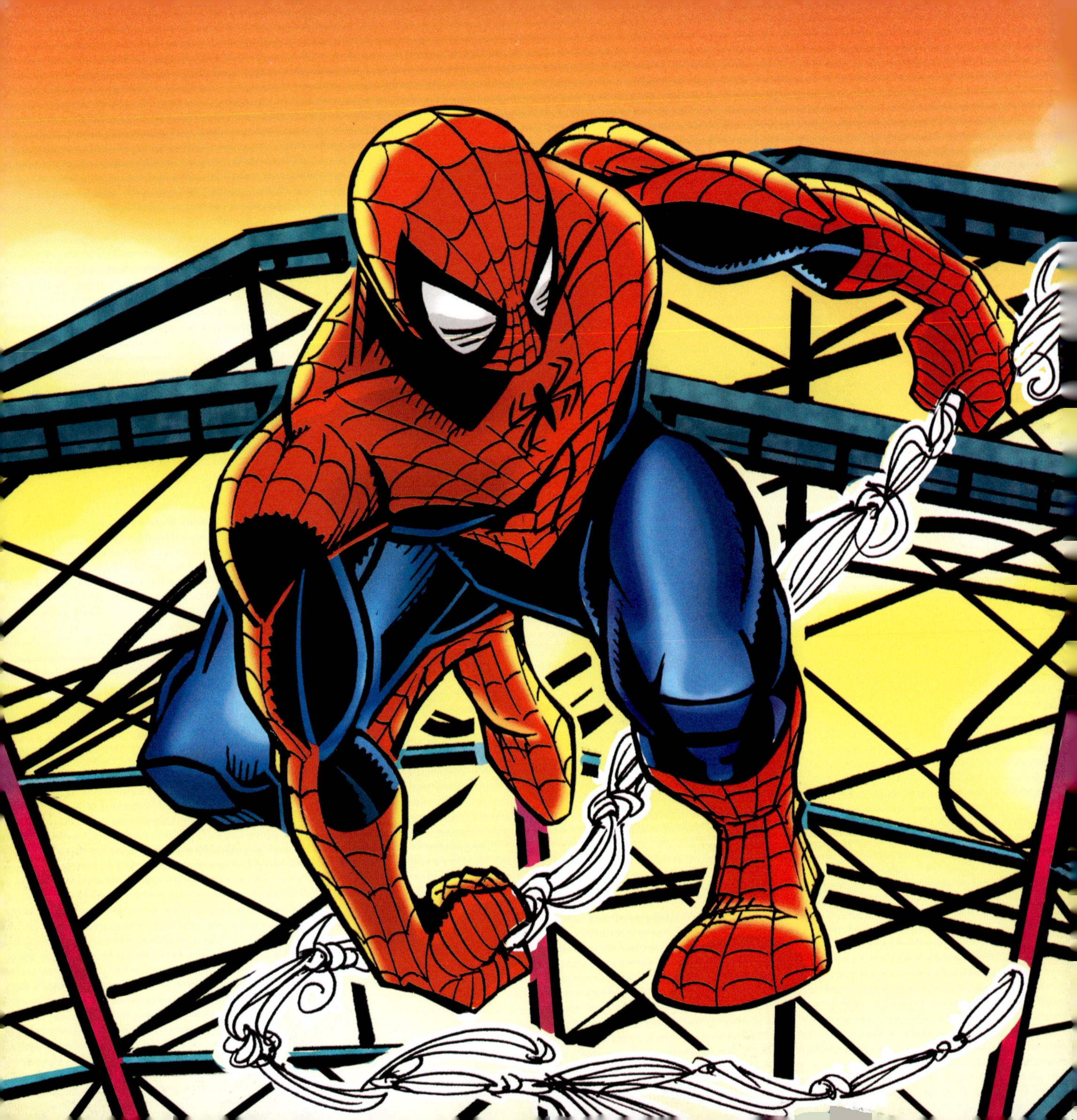

Sandman will never get me up here, Spider-Man thought, swinging to the top of the Ferris wheel. *Now, I've got to figure out how to stop him!*

"You can't run away, Spider-Man!" bellowed Sandman as he shot two beams of sand at the Ferris wheel and then hardened them. He began to turn the giant wheel, using his now hard-as-concrete arms.

"This ride's no fun," Spider-Man called out as he leapt from the creaking wheel.

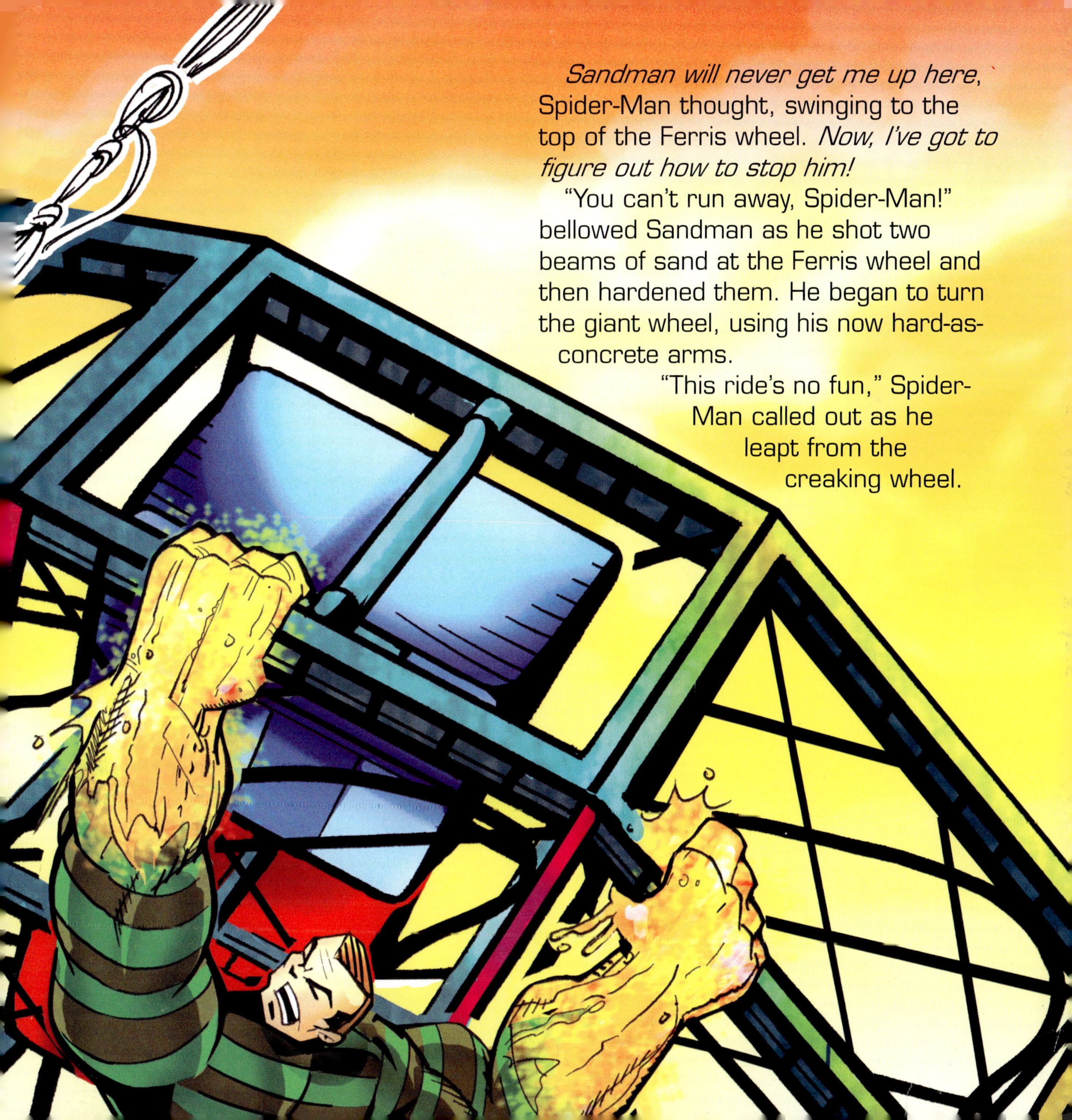

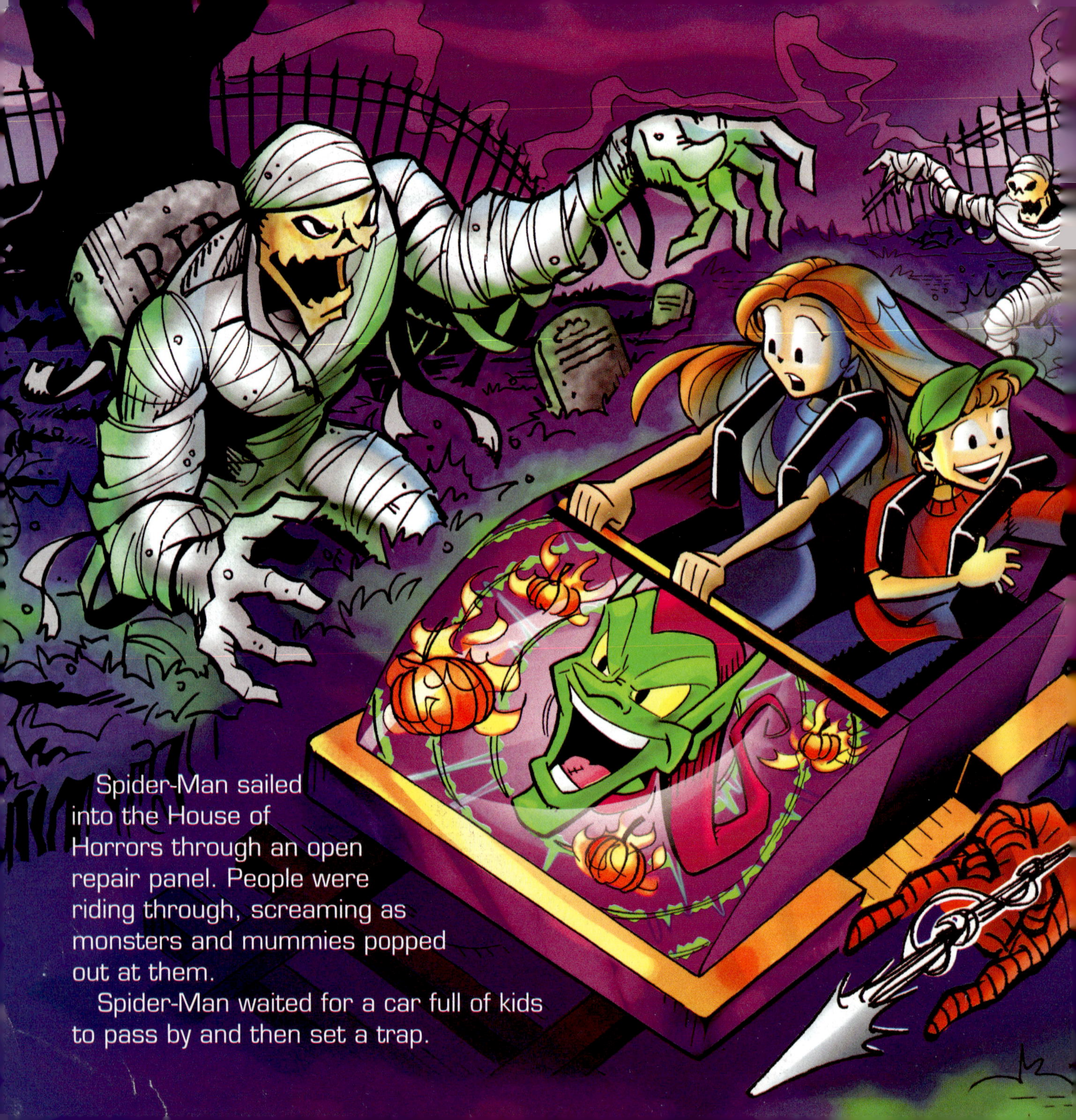

Spider-Man sailed into the House of Horrors through an open repair panel. People were riding through, screaming as monsters and mummies popped out at them.

Spider-Man waited for a car full of kids to pass by and then set a trap.

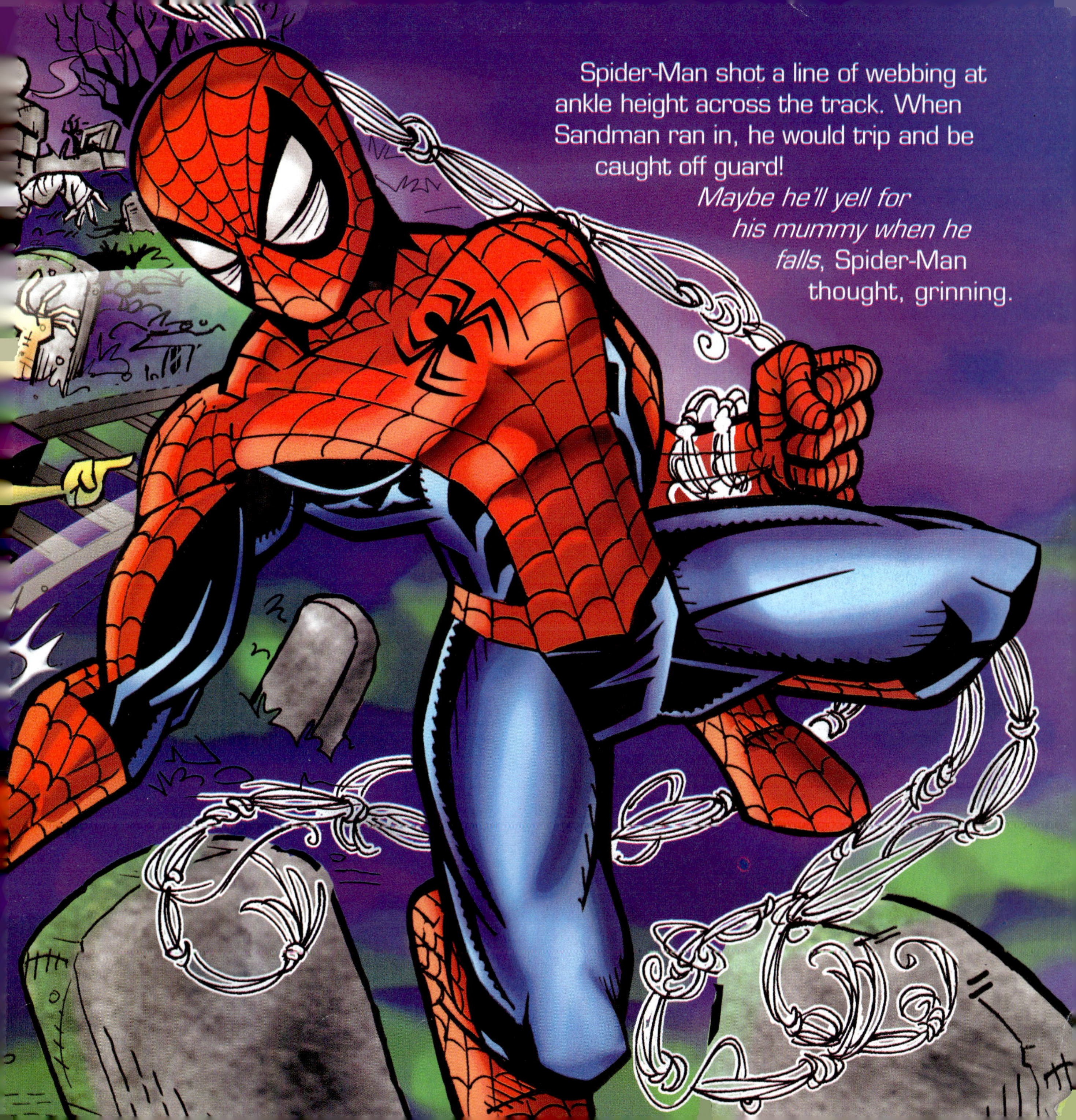

Spider-Man shot a line of webbing at ankle height across the track. When Sandman ran in, he would trip and be caught off guard!

Maybe he'll yell for his mummy when he falls, Spider-Man thought, grinning.

"Where are you, Spider-Man? I know you're in here!" Sandman shouted, running into the House of Horrors. He was madder than ever! Sandman turned the corner and saw Spider-Man—but suddenly he tripped over something as he raced toward the Webbed One.

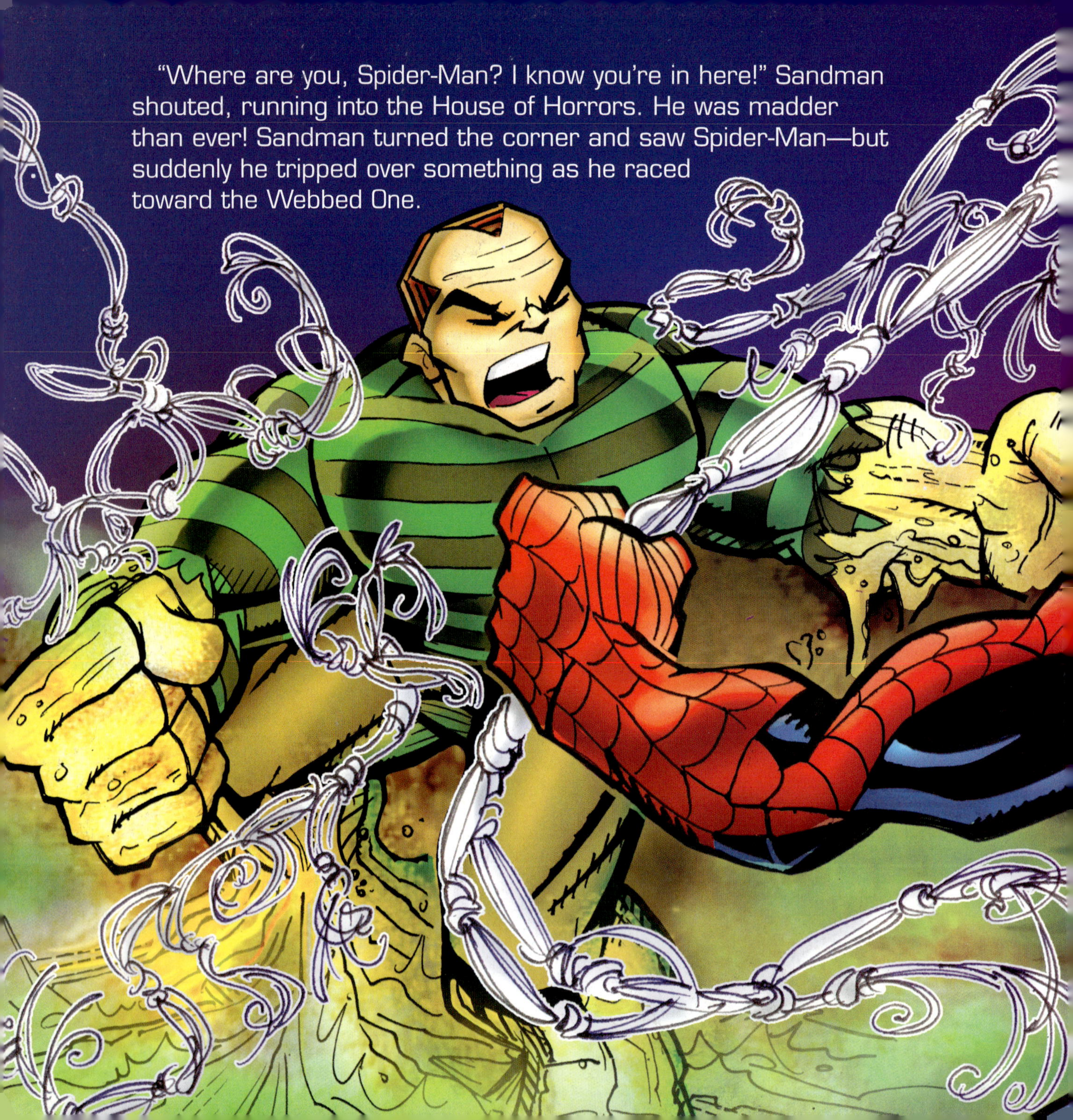

SPLAT! Sandman crashed to the tracks and exploded into a giant pile of sand!

Spider-Man covered the pile of sand that used to be Sandman with a web, but he knew it wouldn't hold Sandy for long.

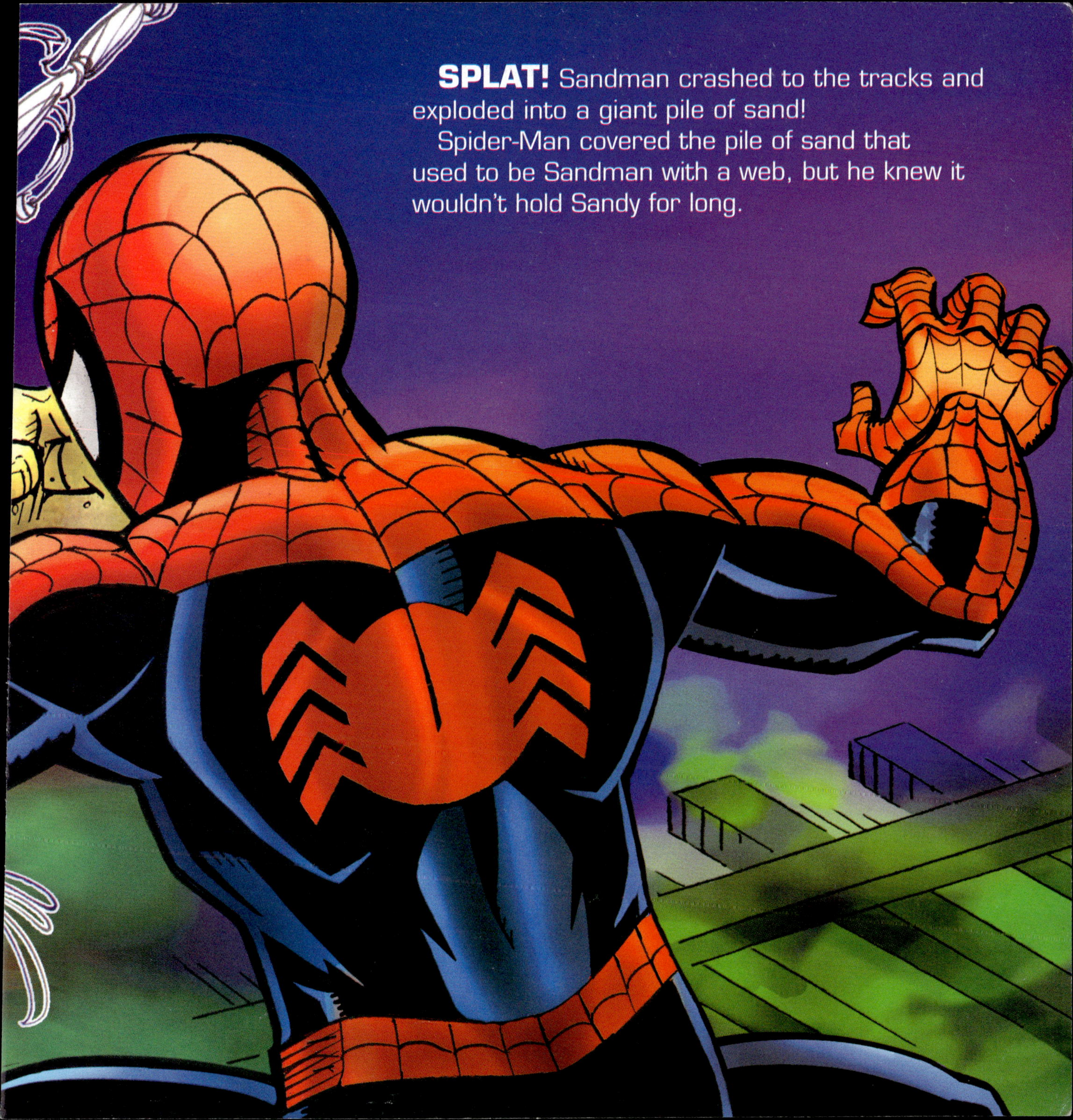

"You've got to do better than that, Webhead," Sandman said, pouring through the gaps of the web.

Spider-Man raced out of the House of Horrors. He had to think fast—Sandman was no ordinary enemy. He had to find something, some way to trap Sandman so he could hand him over to the police. But how?

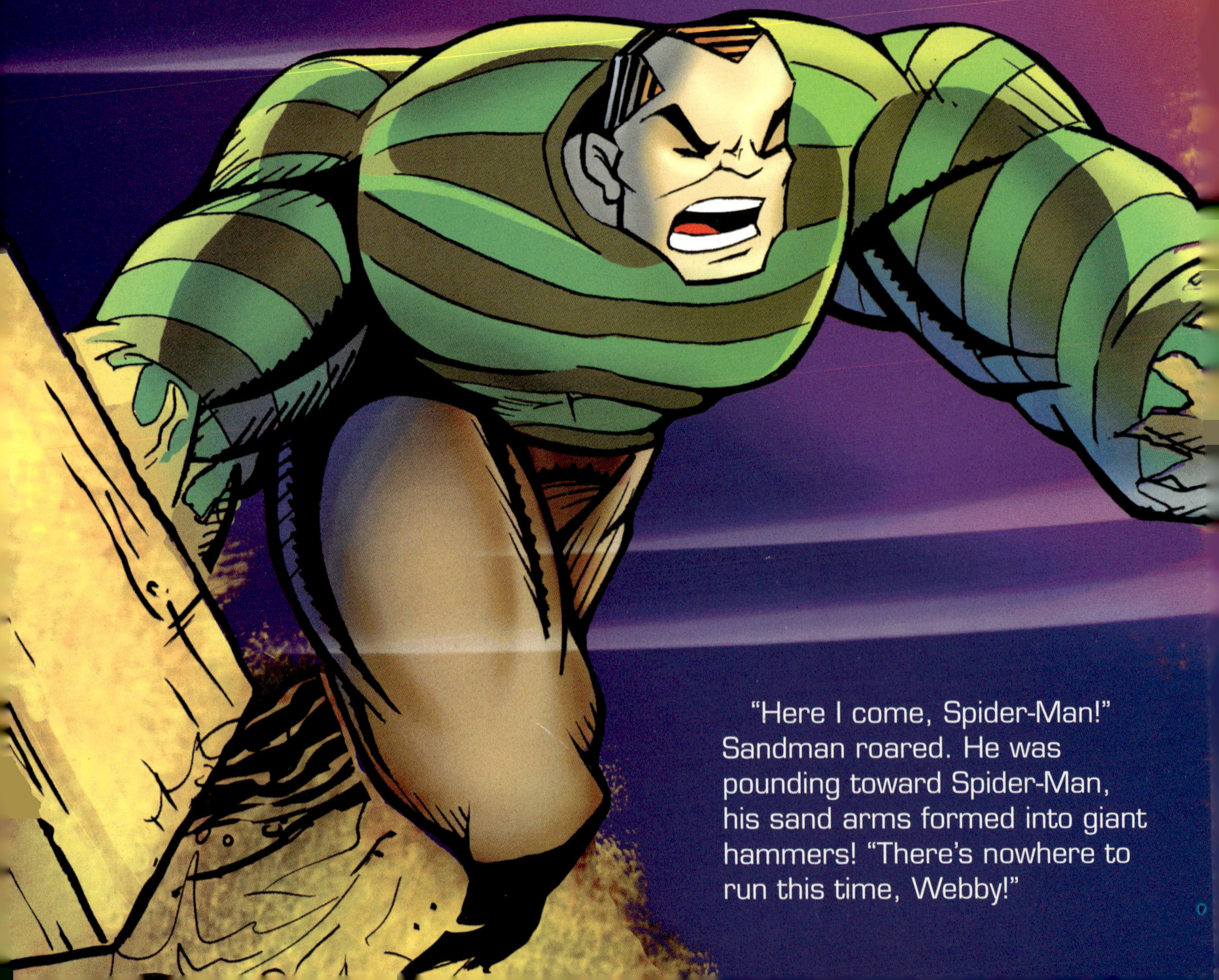

"Here I come, Spider-Man!" Sandman roared. He was pounding toward Spider-Man, his sand arms formed into giant hammers! "There's nowhere to run this time, Webby!"

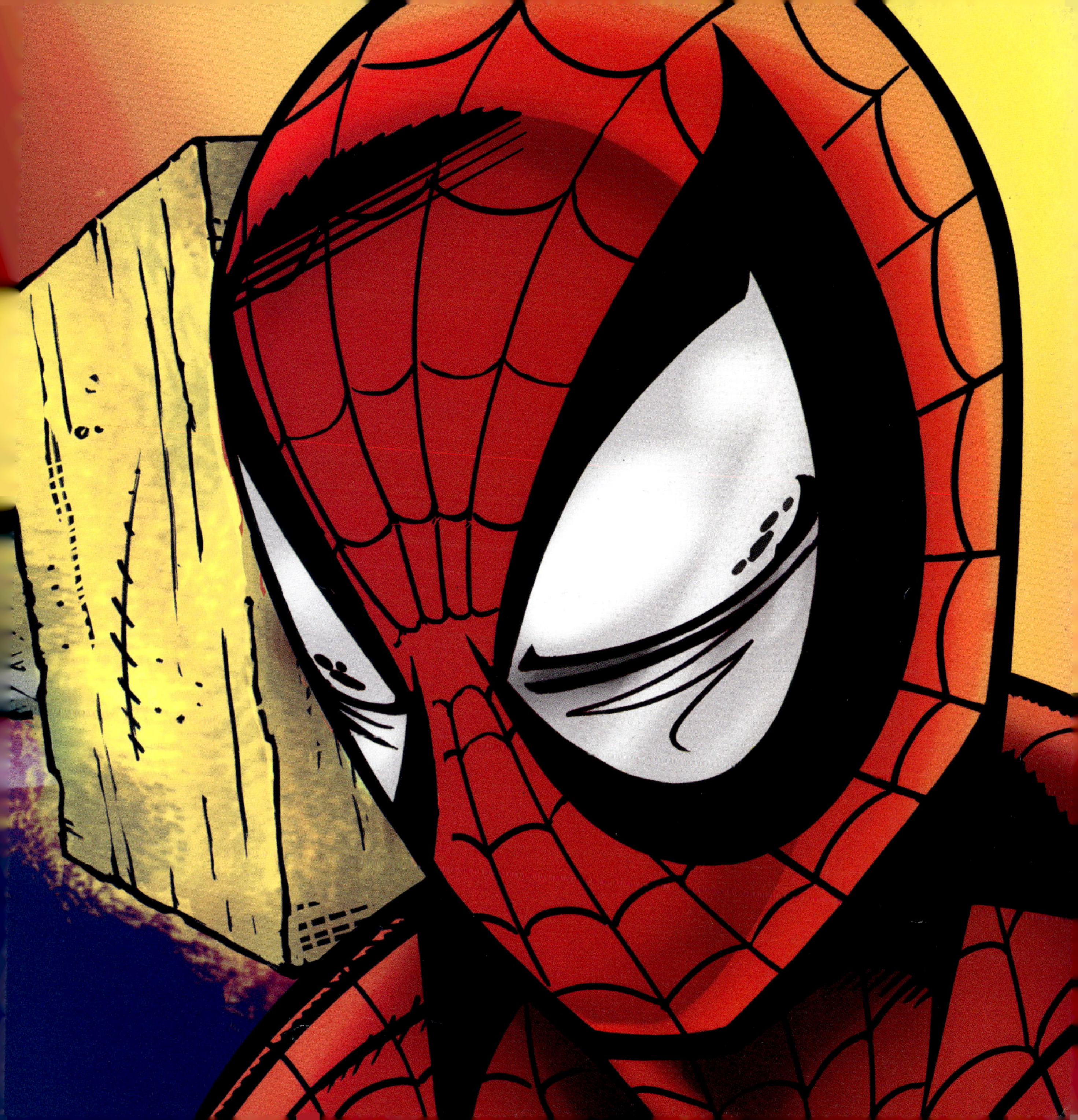

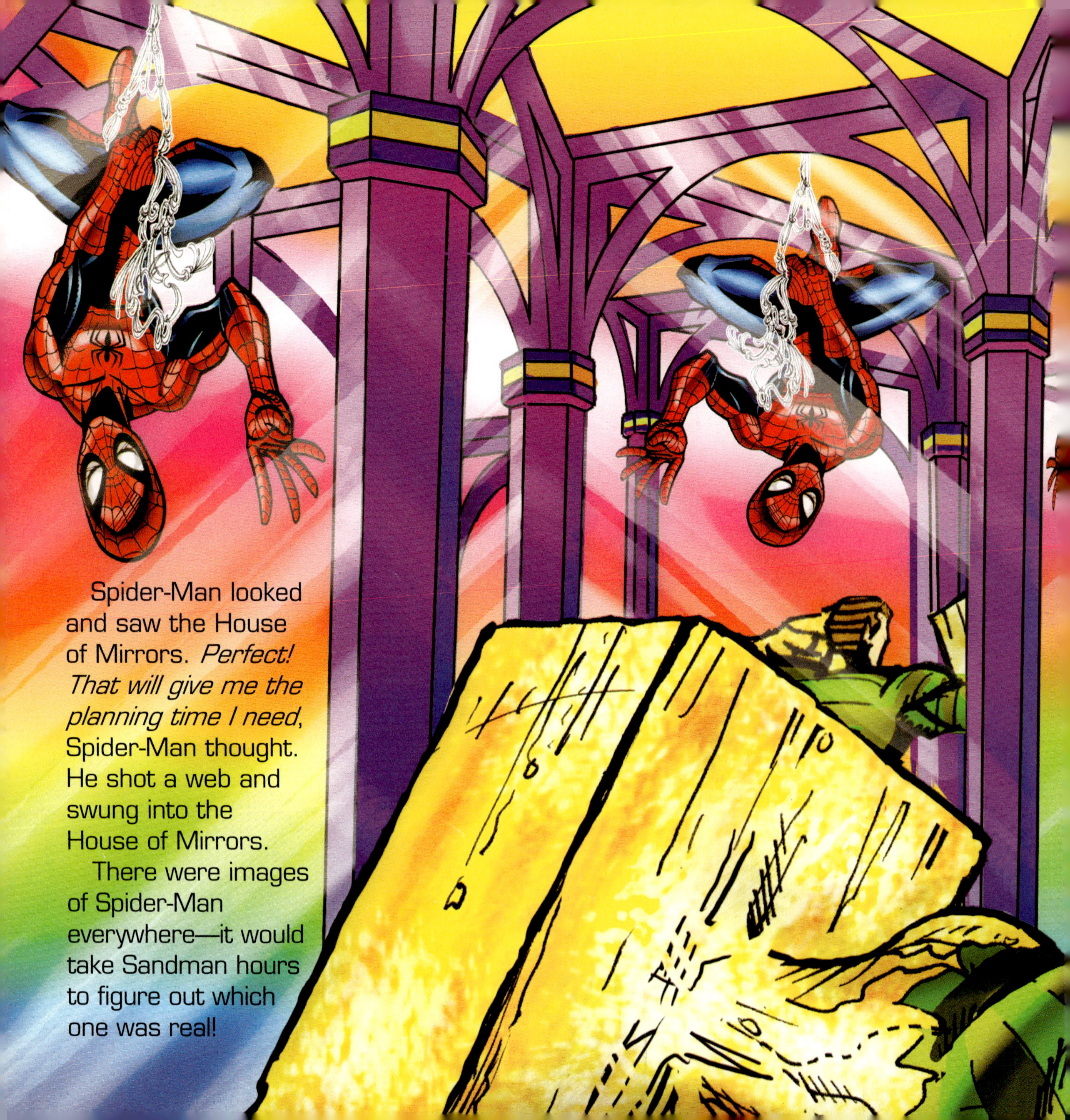

Spider-Man looked and saw the House of Mirrors. *Perfect! That will give me the planning time I need*, Spider-Man thought. He shot a web and swung into the House of Mirrors.

There were images of Spider-Man everywhere—it would take Sandman hours to figure out which one was real!

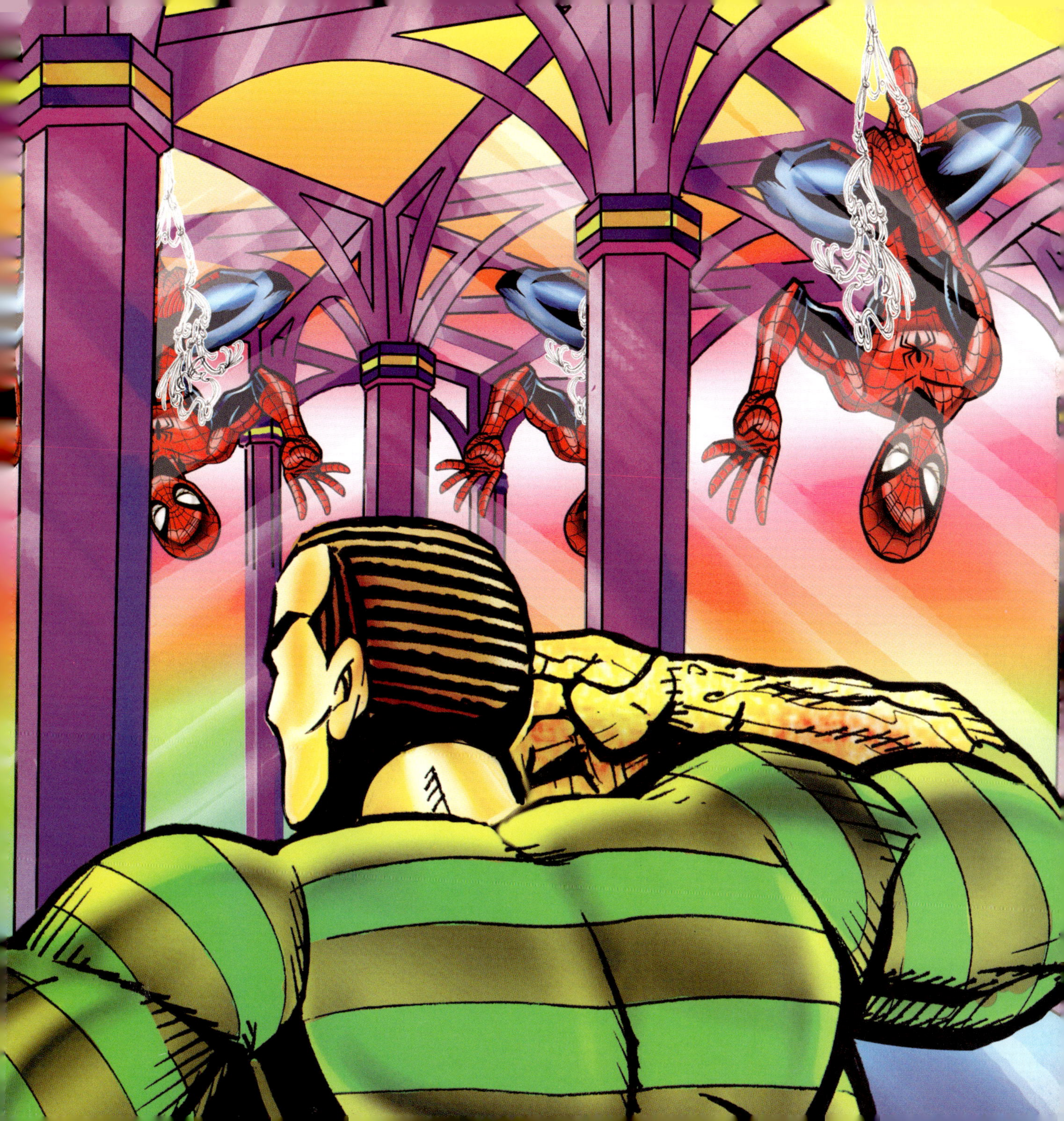

"You can't fool me, Spider-Man!" Sandman said, laughing and running into the House of Mirrors. "I'll shatter you!" Sandman slammed mirror after mirror with his hammer-shaped arms, shattering the images of Spider-Man one by one.

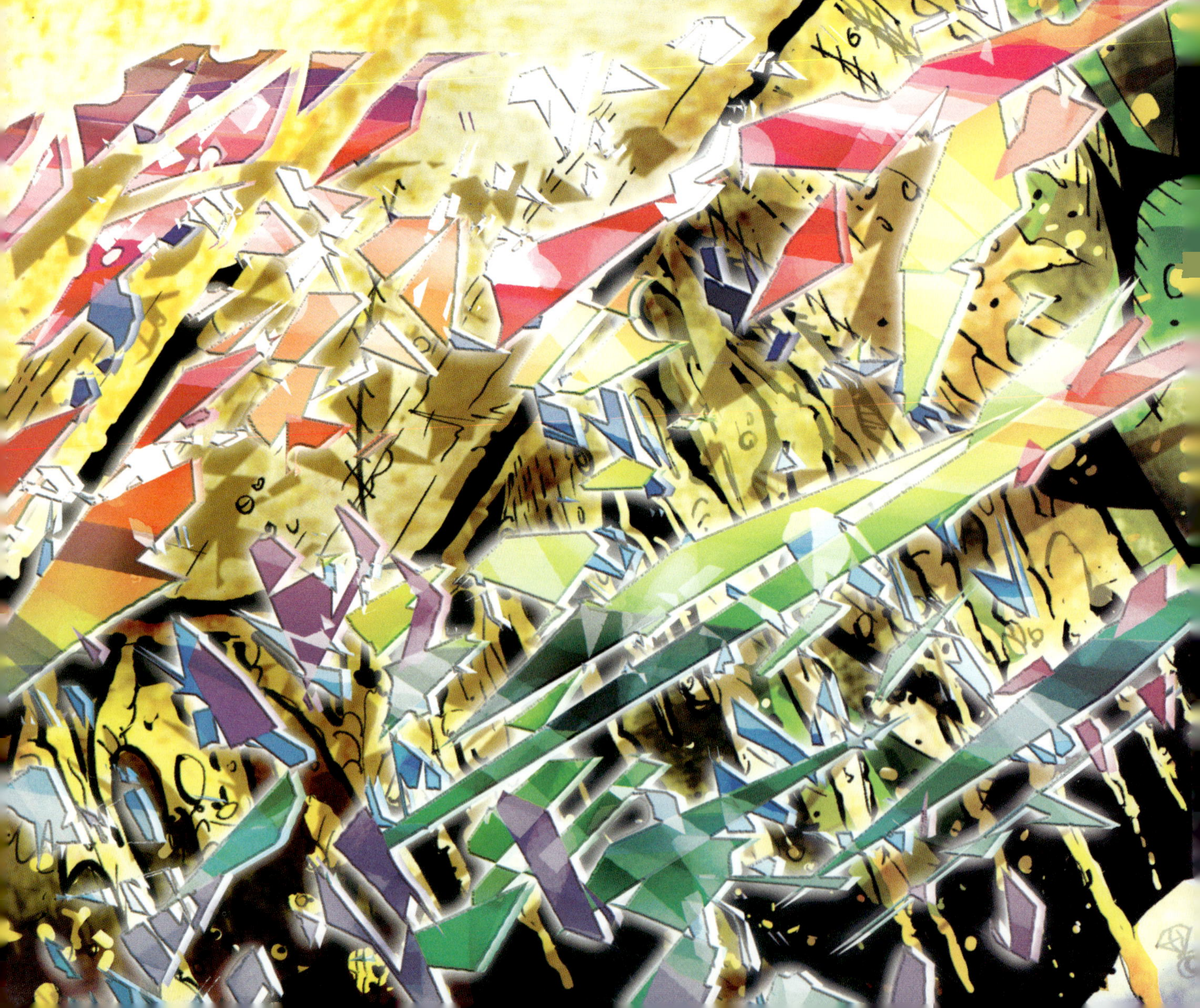

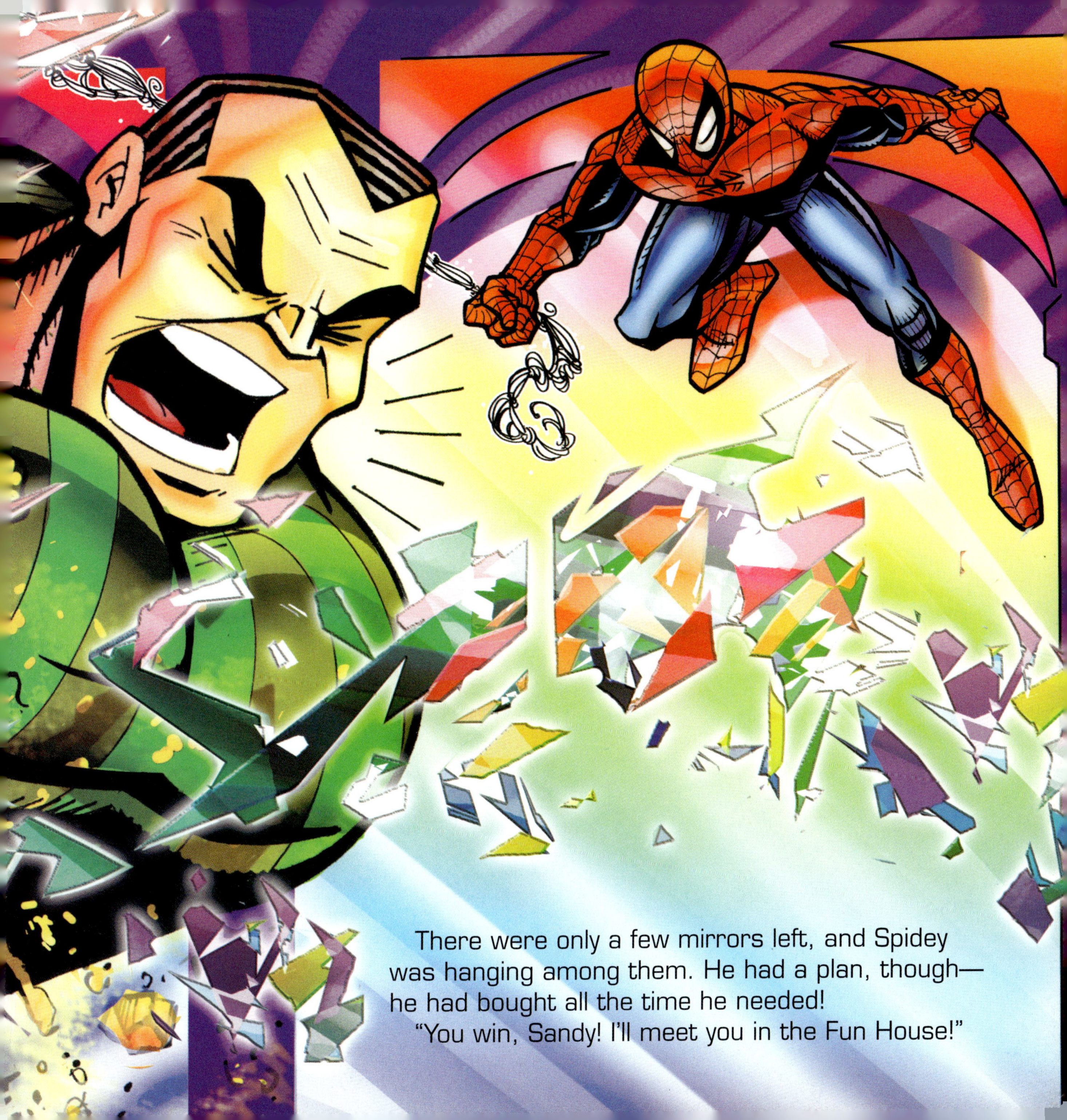

There were only a few mirrors left, and Spidey was hanging among them. He had a plan, though—he had bought all the time he needed!

"You win, Sandy! I'll meet you in the Fun House!"

Spider-Man had to act quickly. He had seen some construction going on around the Fun House. Into the Fun House he swung, shooting webbing to slow Sandman.

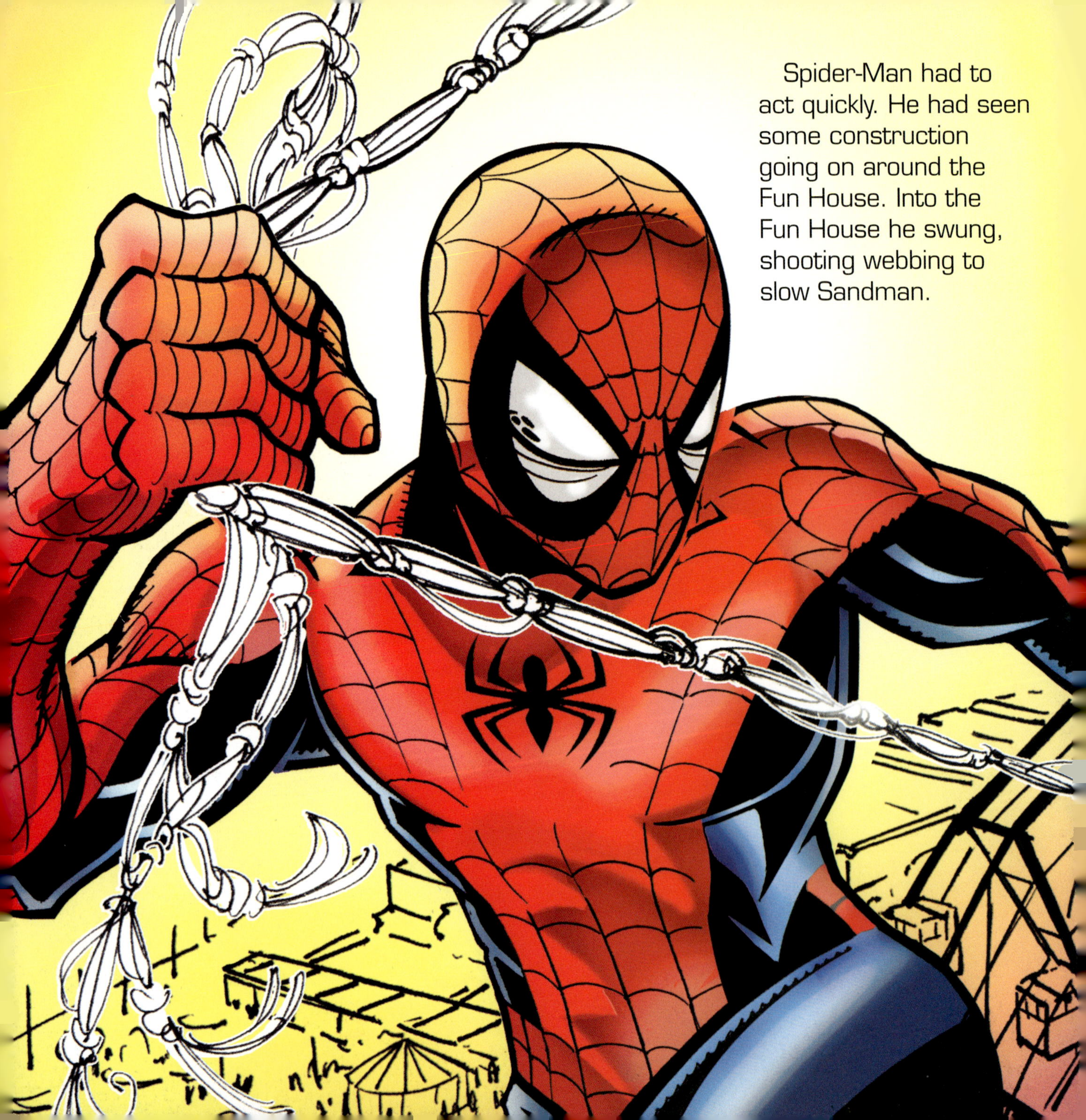

At the other end of the Fun House, Spidey jumped out a window and onto a cement mixer. Thinking fast, he pushed the mixer in front of the Turning Tunnel—a spinning tunnel people try to walk through without falling. Then Spider-Man yelled at Sandman from the other side.

When Spider-Man heard Sandman rush into the tunnel, he turned on the cement mixer at the other end. Seeing the mixer too late, Sandman stumbled and landed headfirst in with the churning cement! Spider-Man slammed the lid.

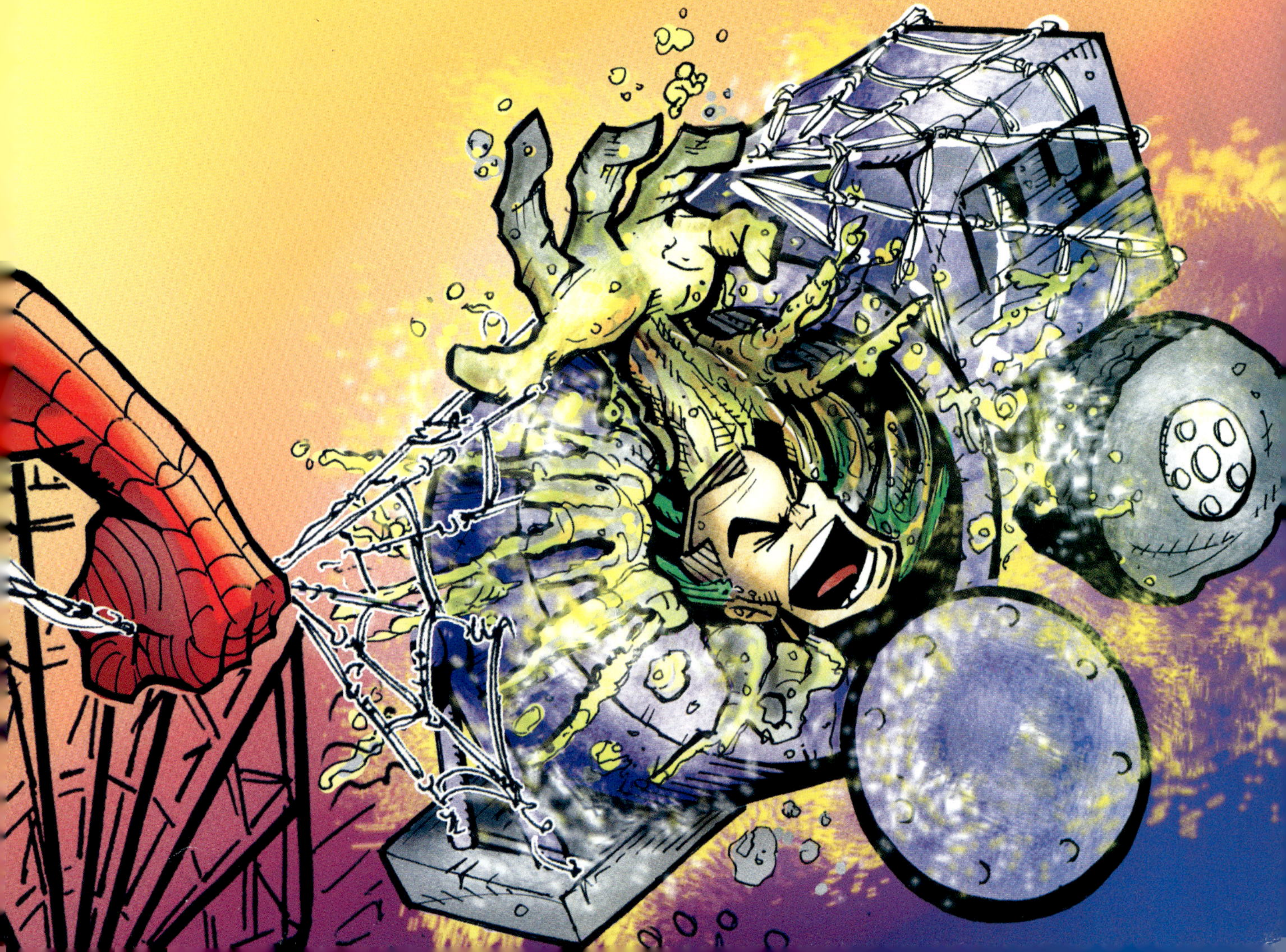

"Sorry about the mix-up, Sandy," Spider-Man said as the police were taking Sandman away. "But you'll have plenty of time to pick yourself apart in prison!"

Spider-Man had defeated Sandman once again—now he had to get to the *Daily Bugle* with those fashion show pictures!

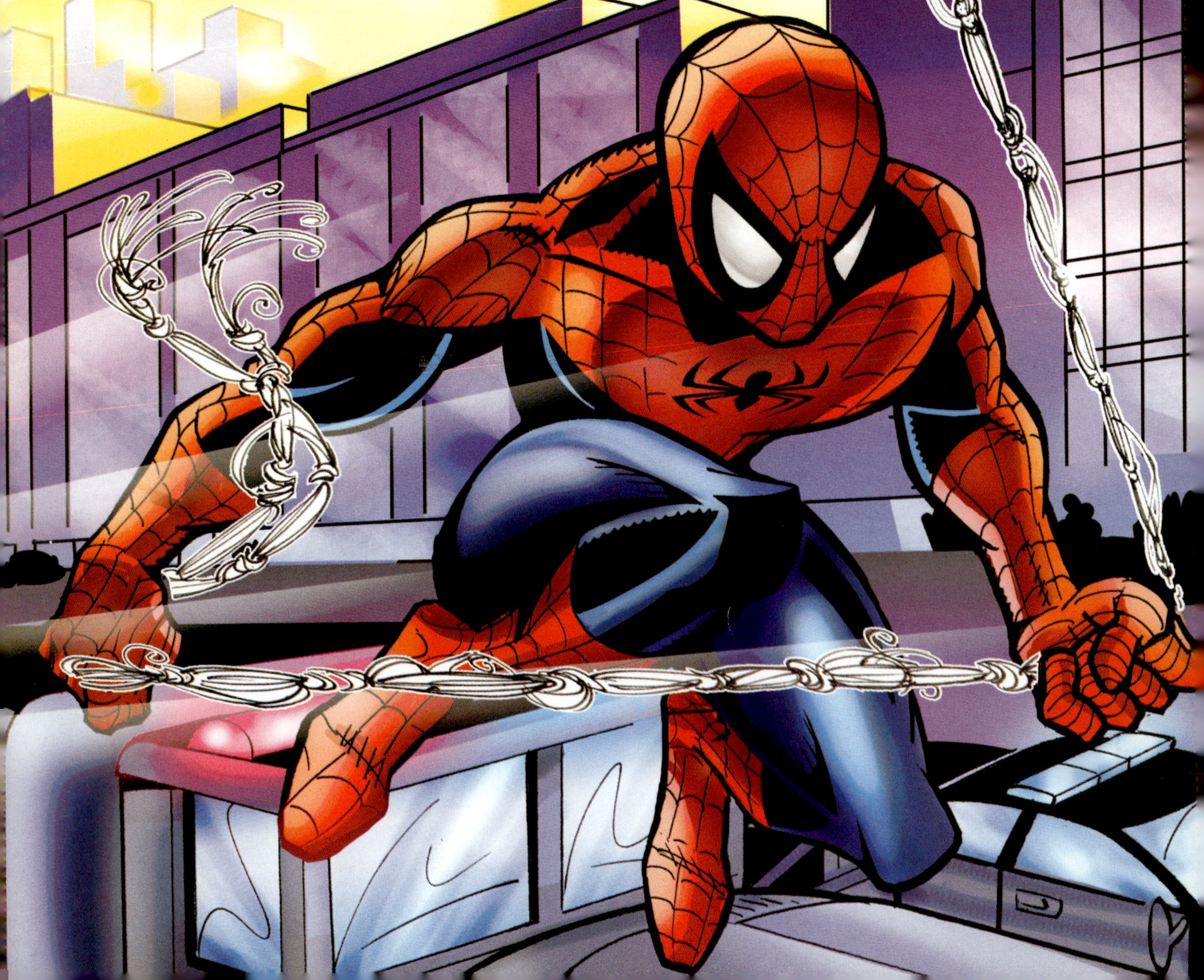